WORLD
WITHOUT END

WORLD WITHOUT END

By

J D Philip Ph.D.

JosephinePublishingPress.com Philadelphia-New Jersey-

Florida-Zambia

FJ GS HE>1

Any comments, recommendations, or suggestions please email us at

charpubpress@aol.com

ISBN:
978-1-329-18649-1

DEDICATION

To the author of the Word.

World Without End

"Here's pop-pop's scrapbook Joseph." Jen
and her husband sat in the basement kitchen of
her grandparents' home. The table, an old
Victorian oak, fed many generations of
Richardsons. If the well patinated grain could
talk, the dark veins would speak to many
divergent conversations. 344 West Burk Ave.
had, at one time, been a single story dwelling.
After having attic dormers installed and raising
the entire home 12 concrete blocks high, the
structure grew to three levels. Even with the
renovations, the home still had a certain cozy
charm created by the matron of the house,
Nanny.

Wild horses still ran through the tall reeds of
the back bay's which surrounded this quaint
community. The oceans roar, just three blocks
east of the home, could be better heard from
the attic converted bedrooms, 35 feet above
ground. Joseph sat, flipping through the now
foxed pages, reading the many poems, notes,

and newspaper clippings that littered the once white construction paper album leaves.

"Jen. The news of today would have been unthinkable before world war two. The information would've been science fiction – like."

The wife answered. "Tell me about it! America and Britain were the power nations, on the verge of smashing the Rome Berlin axis. Look at us today. England has been shorn of her empire and American lives in a state of moral and cultural decay."

"You always were one for astute political science insight my wife. It appears that the nations we defeated back then have now joined forces under that so-called farcical European Union which appears to be dominated by the Germans," stated jol.

"What I can't understand, with the shrinking of the world, it being so intertwined and interconnected, how can the globe have become more divided and fragmentary? We've gone back to the old ethnic and religious lines of demarcation!" Jen had a great point which made the pedagogue think.

"All I know is that hatred abounds among old ancient lines and has been renewed afresh," commented jol.

"You can feel it too? How the ire, rancor, and vileness has penetrated, corrupted, and become an evil miasma that covers a planet."

As the two spoke, daughter Elizabeth and the two grandchildren came bursting into the first floor.

"Gigi! Bob! Something's weird outside."

"Yeah mom. The sky is bleeding... Dad, I'm not crazy, the sky is full of blood!"

"It is Bob," shouted AJ and Jojo.

Joseph, a.k.a. Bob to the daughter and grandkids, looked out the side window near the workbench. He said quietly to himself, "it's finally happening. Human emotions, the greed, the pride, selfishness, lack of belief has finally channeled the world into a different path. The entire global structure has finally fractured." Bob recalled explaining this to his students, when he taught at the University of Zambia.

"Our humanity seeks an identity that far out reaches our current divisions and rivalries. We are at the brink of a world that will not be able to be understood. The mind, in corporate union, will one day supplant our world of peace with chaos and lifeforms that will terrorize our human core! Then, at the time when our group indulgence centers on self-materializing we will pray for faceless beings. For what we will see will turn our hearts and souls to ice, our spirits to hate, and our minds to confusion toward all that we once loved. At the dénouement there will be only one answer to our plight.

One source and one source only can find a solution. The mysterious beast with heads and horns, slime and decay, and an evilness beyond hell will mark us well. The monstrosities will dominate and control the entire world. The awesome power and grip that the vile abnormalities possess will shackle us like prisoners on a sinking Roman galley. My dear students, please take heed to these prophetic words. Listen to what I have to say. Hear if you wish. These statements will have a profound effect on your world and your future, more so than you can fathom. They do ring true. They will constitute your reality in the not so distant future."

Dr. jol's students sat on the edge of their lecture hall seats. Their eyes were widened as much as their ears drew into hear. The professor spoke only when need be, and then, only in brief fact. On the rare occurrence of one of his extended discourses, student tradition knew that his words contained substance.

"Dr. jol how can you be so sure about your prognosis?" asked a second year medical student.

"Ahhh... Good!... Very good!... You do not accept words of man alone. We've taught you well. Never listen and follow without thought, evaluation, and testing. If it makes sense, it probably is. But to your answer, Zimbabwe! Many of us remember it as Southern Rhodesia, a few as central Africa or the Congo." The professor sat behind his podium staring up at the amphitheater tiers which seated 300 eager, attentive, and impressionable minds. Dr. jol always ensured that what he said could be taken to the "bank"!

"Just as you look upon me now, back then, in prehistory all eyes turned to an elderly man as he walked erect, into the bright oil lamp lit and lavishly decorated great rondoval hall. Just an hour before the old man's arrival, the banquet room had been bustling with music, dance, eating, banter, and wine-induced revelry. Suddenly, in a blink, the cacophony quelled to an eerie cold silence as if death had arrived and taken hold of the celebration.

A spine chilling scene had frozen each guest in their places with only the slightest hint of nervous whispering being discerned, bordering on terror to some degree. One brave soul, white as white could be from a brush with horror, shouted out in disbelief; maybe to confirm what his eyes may have deceived.

'A hand! Only a bloodstained hand from cut wrist to fingertips! From the air! Out of nowhere! Look! Over here! On the wall!'

The guests could not turn their heads. Paralyzing fear only permitted them to shift their eyes to the wall that had been pointed out by the now collapsed, panic stricken, and very dead spokesman."

jol paused briefly. Some students bit their bottom lips gnawing on the puff of flesh. Others wide-eyed even more, the lecture had taken on the ambience of the banquet hall of which the professor spoke; hearts beat rapidly, minds raced, imaginations played tricks.

"The occasion, yes, the reason for the great feast. The fete had been planned by King Nemfukwe, the ruler of all the lands as far as his runners could stride. The celebration, to reward his people for building a wall so powerful and huge, that it made the now modern country of Zimbabwe invincible.

'This feat that you have accomplished, my people, makes our domain impregnable. Ours is a land of plenty, yes a land that's good and plenty, of strength, of safety. Even King Febe and his mighty warriors had given up their attacks. That ruthless and relentless ruler never despairs, being like one of our ridge back canines. Yes my people, even Febe ran like a scared jackal.'"

"Professor, I recall studying the incident of which you spoke, in Dr. Ida's archaeology class. I believe the year of that event to be 539 BC."

"Very observant Tembo. You are following in Doctor Ida's footsteps I take it?"

"Yes Dr, jol, it may take me a lifetime to fill one of her sandals but she has been a tremendous inspiration and light in our field," responded Tembo.

"And what else can you recall of those events?" asked jol.

"The new moon. The seventh month. Doctor Ida called that the number of completion. And the words 'MENE, MENE, TEKEL, UPHARSIN.'"

"Well done my good Miss Tembo. Most astute and accurate and factual. My sister, the professor, has done her usual thorough job in instruction. I know she told the story of Nemfukwe and the wall, for she has excavated much of the Zimbabwe ruins. But the story bears repeating for the many who do not know the facts, not yet having the opportunity to sit in my sister's class.

The elite of the Congoan kingdom gathered that night to celebrate, drink, and toast the Great Wall. The chibuku flowed freely. Thousands of gourds of the mead had been recently brewed for the event. King Nemfukwe insisted on using the sacred vessels that had been captured in past battles, booty if you will, to be used as drinking goblets. The solid gold jewel encrusted containers overflowed with drink. Words of praise were foisted upon the chief of Zimbabwe and his people, by all the visitors and guests in attendance.

All stood right with the countryside. Then, from the midst of the pyre smoke appeared the hand, writing upon the dung stuccoed stone walls in crimson lettering. The entire festival came to an abruptly stunned halt. All fell silent. Those words that Miss Tembo just mentioned inscribed the King's wall, 'MENE, MENE, TEKEL, UPHARSIN.' They were not well known to the guests, but were very familiar to the evil forces that lurked outside of Chief Nemfukwe's wall."

"Professor if I may," interrupted David the economics major. "Those are units of ancient weight, if I'm not mistaken."

"Excellent and most true. You know that. I know that. Their significance at the time were utterly incomprehensible to those at the banquet. That leads us back to the ancient man whom all stared at, as he walked in the presence of the king's candelabrum lights. The Chief summoned Daka from out of the shadows. The old man had been brought to Nemfukwe's court as a teenaged Fulani captive. Daka had risen to high office under Nemfukwe's grandfather, Nemfukwe the Elder, and had gained much prowess in the kingdom during the early years.

Daka did not wish such magnanimous treatment, being a humble man. A power moved him, therefore he gave praise to that Entity. Being who he was, an obedient servant, Daka remained faithful to the Voice that directed his mission in life.

'Daka!' called Nemfukwe the Younger. 'What meaning do these words have in interrupting our celebration and scaring my guests half to death?'

Daka examined the writings. 'My great King. Our Creator, the one who rules even over you, has numbered your kingdom. It has neared its end. You have, in His all-knowing mind and benevolent heart, been weighed in the balance. He has found you wanting.' The words of Daka incensed Nemfukwe. They were prophetic and quick.

That very night the Puku and Lozi tribes invaded the Chief's city, besieging and pillaging. I'll have my graduate assistant, Mister Robert continue."

"Thank you Dr. Jol. The younger Nemfukwe had a grand scheme with building the wall. The King knew that the height was too large to scale and the girth too massive to penetrate. He underestimated the creativity of those who live in the bush studying the moles of the continent. The underpinning of the great stone barrier lacked. The Puku and the Lozi saw its vulnerability being built upon soft earth.

Furthermore, for a fresh water supply, Nemfukwe had a canal built off the Zambezi River running below and beneath the city wall. Once diverted by the two attacking tribes, the canal dried and provided a direct tunnel beneath the Great Wall. In the dark of the predawn hours, the Lozi and Puku, with spears and shields in hand, marched through the dry riverbed and opened the massive ironwood gates from the inside of the Chief's kingdom.

The King's men attempted to defend the city. Assagais were too much for them. The short stabbing spears, with extra-large blades butchered the Zimbabweans. Seme wounds caused blood to flow like the great African rivers. Knobkerries crushed skulls like women opening ostrich eggs for meal preparation. Before sunrise the Lozi and Puku conquered the city and executed King Nemfukwe with his own seme, the sword passed down to him by his great-grandfather.

The city stood in chaos. Fire and smoke filled every hut. Blood ran as freely as the once flowing stream of fresh drinking water. The smell of death choked the living. Bodies were stepping stones used to flee the carnage for some Zimbabweans. The wealthy were taken in chains in order to fill the slave quota. Screams with cries of pain and suffering replaced the party atmosphere of the night before.

Daka, confronted by the previous evening's events, lay in his rope bed reflecting. For some odd reason, by the hand of his Maker, the infidels that ravaged the South Central Congo region did not trouble themselves with certain captives; Daka being one of the untouched. Can anyone in class conjecture why that was so?" Mister Robert posed an interesting question to the students. "Anyone?... Yes, Miss Reynolds."

"I believe that, just as the forces of evil infiltrated the compound of Nemfukwe, those powers of good had a protective shield surrounding Daka and those who were of the same ilk."

"Perfectly sound reasoning," chimed in jol. "The man, being well into his 80s probably seemed useless to the two attacking tribes. The Lozi and Puku had no idea of his prowess with prophecy, dream interpretation, and heavenly realms. Daka, as Robert explained, contemplated a brief confrontation. His mind flashed back 65 years.

'You have been brought before me, 'spoke Chief Nemfukwe's grandfather," explained Dr. jol. The professor continued the tale of the teen years of Daka.

"The story of the prophet continues in the court of Nemfukwe the Elder.

'You have been brought into the presence of the ruler of the most powerful country on this earth. Your life, and the lives of your compatriots, hang from a thread. Work well and live! Falter and die.' The king was most serious.

That's how the elder chief approached the new Fulani slave. Nemfukwe the Elder had been having a series of baffling dreams which caused him distress. No one could decipher their meaning.

Daka, upon hearing the King ordered the execution of two of his dream interpreters for false information, knew that he himself had a special gift.

'King! King! Please allow me to assist,' spoke Daka pulling away from the guards who held him.

'Who dares address the Chief without first being acknowledged? That boldness has saved you from instant death young slave. Allow him to pass.' While standing in front of him the King eyed the youth for some minutes. 'A bold one we have here!'

The guards knew to what the King referred. They knocked Daka to his knees, held down his shoulders and forced his gaze to the dirt. 'Now you may speak sassy one.'

'Meaning no disrespect King, I overheard your need. I have been gifted from Him who resides above, with the ability to reveal one's most intimate thoughts which are shown during sleep. The Father has spoken to me on many occasions concerning the symbols that run through our minds while our eyes seek rest.'

'You are a bold one. I have the most reliable and respected and wise of all dream readers and you, an impish, dirty faced slave can outdo my experts?' The Chief posed a powerful question to the young man.

'I can! I will! You'll see. The One who speaks to and through me reveals all. There are no secrets in that realm in which He exists. He has prepared me by my fasting, special diet, wisdom keeping, revelation, and meditative prayer to read visions and dreams. Test me if you must. If you have the courage to know truth. Provide me an opportunity to prove my worth. You can always dispose of me if my words do not match the ability of which I speak.'

The ruler broke out into a huge smirk. 'A bold one indeed. I shall. If you falter, you die!' The Chief began to explain the series of events which surrounded his first puzzling dream. 'One night I awoke from a disturbing vision. I called for my magicians, enchanters, sorcerers, and astrologers. I asked them about the night images I had and insisted on finding their meanings.

One of my sorcerers could only say, 'Long live Nemfukwe.'

He asked me to provide him the details of my dream. Then and only then would he give me its meaning. I became enraged, I explained to the fool that this dream did not contain idiocy, but was a most serious concern of mine. I demanded that he tell me the dream at once. I provided the options for if he did or did not speak the truth. The sorcerer's words were foolish. Instead of rewards from the king's treasure, I ordered for him to be tossed in the crocodile pit. The one most hungry and brutal ripped him limb from limb. His many morsels of flesh satisfied my brood.

Next I spoke with one of my astrologers. You would've thought word of the crocodile's meal would have sharpened his skills. He begged me to tell him of my dream. Only then could he give me its meaning. Even now, his irritating misguided stupidity causes me to rear up and bellow. I told him that I understood his foolish scheme of stalling for time. He did not realize the astute nature of the Elder. Taking me for a mindless old man I fed him to the cats. He begged me for mercy but lies must be punished.

After the lions finished their repast the magician came to me. He sensed my ire. So he spoke quickly. Do you know what he said to me? No one on this earth, in my kingdom could tell me my dream! The nerve of that man. He continued by implying I asked what no other king has asked, wisdom from the wisdom keepers. They accused me of asking the impossible. Since both had no wisdom, the loss of their heads to the executioner was of little consequence. Now I see I must confront the gods, they have the powers to read one's night visions.

After deciding to find an earthly god to help me, I gave the order, 'execute them all.' They call themselves wise but have no wisdom. 'Kill all my slaves, even that young Daka. The lions arc hungry.'

'Your kingship. I recall that order. The guards gathered us up. I went to your headman to ask a question.' Daka quickly spoke.

'Hakim, why has the king ordered our deaths?'

Hakim explained what had transpired concerning your dreams and your men of wisdom, or lack thereof.

'I can!' I shouted.

'You can what?' Hakim asked me.

'Interpret. Please.' I begged. 'Take me to the Chief.'

At first Hakim refused. 'No! Place them all in chains. We will execute them tomorrow evening when the cat's appetites are most heightened.'

While in the prison kraal I had a strange vision. I slept soundly having confidence in what had been shown me by way of answers to my prayers. With the morning sun I shouted out, 'Hakim, I must speak with the King!'

At early dawn on the day of my scheduled execution Hakim answered, 'under penalty of my own death I do so Daka.'

'When I saw you, the bold one, I drew my seme. You were most fortunate that Hakim is my nephew, the son of my oldest sister. He spoke for you.'

Hakim said, 'I have found one who will speak to your dreams dear Elder, my uncle.'

'The words piqued my interest.'

'But you did not sheath your sword,' remembered Daka. Then you asked me Chief, 'do I know you young lad?'

I answered, 'you and your army attacked Makuni village and captured the entire Fulani populace. Your men took a number of children, including me, back here to your kingdom. We have been schooled, fed, and nurtured on your ways.'

I remember laughing beneath my scowl. 'That means nothing to me. Is it true? You can describe my dream and tell me its significance?'

'None of your court could do so, correct?' I asked. 'But there is One, above us all who reveals secrets. He has shown me what will happen to Nemfukwe the Elder in the future. This has been what the great One revealed to me. And now, here we are at the present, I believe you have accepted my offer of revelation?'

'Falter and you die. Weigh your words very carefully. Death can be the reward for one misplaced phrase.'

Daka took a deep breath and swallowed. 'My King, you dreamed of coming events. A giant bright statue you saw, of a man.'

The Chief shifted to the edge of his royal stool for Daka spoke truth. 'Yes,' said Nemfukwe. 'Continue! I demand it.'

'The head had been cast of fine gold. The upper torso of silver, a belly with thighs of bronze. The legs that you saw were of iron ending in feet of clay.'

The king could not believe the details. Daka's description intrigued the Chief. 'Suddenly you saw a rock mysteriously be cut out from the side of a mountain. The boulder fell toward the statue, smashing the feet to dust.'

The King quieted. He calmed. His mind relaxed for he knew that Daka knew.

'Without a solid base, the monumental figure fell, crumbling into a thousand pieces.'

'True boy. So very very true.'

'The winds began to increase in strength, tornado like, blowing the earth clean like disappearing chaff from wheat. Much to your amazement, the rock that crushed the statue's feet did not leave, but grew into a mountain covering the entire area which had been previously taken up by the enormous mixed metal element figure.'

The King jumped from his royal carved acacia wood throne. He shouted with excitement,' That was the dream! Only I knew its contents. That was the dream in every detail. More, give me more. The meaning. I order it! The meaning.'

'As you know King Nemfukwe the Elder, you are the greatest King upon the continent, no in all the lands. You have been gifted by heaven's main resident and owner with sovereignty, strength, honor, and power. You rule over all that resides in this world. Nature, the animals, the fish that swim the Zambezi come under the reign of the Elder Chief. You are the head of gold.'

The King glowed like the precious metal that symbolized him. The moon could never be brighter than the king's face at that disclosed dream moment, not even on the darkest night upon the savanna plains. Nemfukwe's smile widened as far as the east is from the west. The king's eyes grew as large as that of the lions, who hunt in the dark of night.

'More. I like what I hear. Tell me more!'

'Like all in life my great Chief, the kingdom will come to an end. The cycle of life dictates it to be so. The disappointing reality states that an inferior ruler will take over your kingdom. That reign will not last, as a third takes over, the bronze rule. The fourth will be as strong as iron. It will come and smash all in its path. Just like your seme that crushes and destroys all that it contacts. The last kingdom will be divided as seen by the statue's two feet and ten toes. The strength of each will vary according to size and use. These entities will vie for power. Heaven will look upon the greed and form its own kingdom that will eventually crush all into nothingness. That event has been symbolized by the falling rock you saw which grew into a majestic mountain.'

The king could not believe that the once lowly teen from Makuni village could provide such detail and insight. The elder King threw himself down before Daka.

'My people. You are to burn flamboyant petals to this youth and make sacrifice to him, the man of vision. His Creator has proved to be the most powerful of all the gods we know. Son, you will be rewarded this day. You will be the ruler over all my lands of Kariba.'

The amphitheater at the University of Zambia filled with the buzz of what Professor Jol had just explained. The students were now able to trace the history of the fall of King Nemfukwe the Elder. His lineage brought them up to date to the Elder's grandson.

Mister Robert outlined the succession of usurpers on the PowerPoint screen.

'First we see the armies of King Zulu take over the kingdom of Nemfukwe. Two hundred years later, the Benin invaded Zululand and became rulers. In 333 BC the great forces of the Benin crossed the mighty veldt and destroyed King Zulu's kingdom. Two years lapsed when the Battle of the Nile occurred. The mighty Dinka crossed the great divide, defeating the Benin, the third great world ruling kingdom now took over.

They ruled for about three hundred years. Eventually, the Dogan were swallowed up by the fourth great world empire, the Yoruba. We see, even now, the influence of their god Eshu upon world affairs. Professor, would you like to continue?' asked Robert.

'Surely. As we all know, before Nemfukwe's dream came to fruition, and just as a refresher for us, the Elder constructed a gold statue sixty cubits high placing it at the termini of the Zambezi River as it flows over Mossi a Tunya, the Great Falls of Zimbabwe. Then he sent an edict, by runners and drummers, throughout the land. It said, 'This is the king's command. When the drums sound, bow to the ground to worship my statue. Refusal will result in being tossed to the lions.' The people obeyed with the exception of those from Makuni, Daka's folks.

The Elder's astrologers informed the king about the noncompliance on the part of the Fulani. The men of wisdom told the ruler, 'Long live Nemfukwe. You issued a decree. They pay no attention to you. They must be punished.'

The King flew into a rage. 'Bring those who refuse to bow to the statue before me.' When they were brought in, the ruler noticed that Daka was among them. 'Is it true? You refuse to serve my gods, to worship my image? I will provide you with one more opportunity to pay homage. Drums! Sound the drums! If you refuse now, you'll be fed to the cats.'

'We refuse,' the group stated in unison.

Then Daka spoke, 'our Maker will protect us from your beasts, the same who has given you answers to your dreams. We will never serve your gods or prostrate to your golden image.'

The King thought for a moment. He knew the power of the interpreters and that of the dreams' interpretations. The One who filled Daka's mouth with the explanations had tremendous strength over all the land.

'Ready the lions,' the King ordered. Nemfukwe's Royal Warriors bound the Fulani, dragged them to the pits, and threw the entirety into the huge earthen caverns. The King peered into the largest of the wells. 'They were bound,' explained the King. 'Look! The chains have been loosed. Those traitors have been freed by some mystical power. They caress the lions' manes and the beasts lick their faces. You!' The King pointed to two of his bodyguards.

'Enter.' The Royal guards did as the chief command. The lions ravaged the two huge men then began to playfully frolic, once again, with Daka and the Fulani.

'Their God is powerful. Bring them up. If any man, woman, or child speaks ill of Daka or his God, they, the vile tongued will be torn limb from limb. I elevate the Fulani to court elders. No harm will ever come to you!'

As time passed, Daka and the Fulani enjoyed the many privileges that were ordered them by the elder King Nemfukwe. His kingdom became theirs. Then, one night the chief had another troubling dream.

He went to Daka. 'My good Chief, what did you see? Or do you wish for me to relay the vision to you again as I did your other dreams?'

'I saw a large tree in the center of our earth. The plant eventually grew to the heavens for all the earth to see. The leaves were deep green, full of fruit, and the animals of the earth lived beneath its shade. Birds speckled the limbs like the spots of a leopard. The music they made sweetened the dry summer sun. The entire inhabitants of Earth ate from the mopane tree's abundance.'

Daka interrupted. 'A voice you heard?'

'Yes Daka. You know, like before, don't you?' The King waited with great anticipation.

'I do King. The voice implored you to cut down the tree, remove all the branches, shake off the leaves, and scatter the fruit. The animals are to be driven away as well as the birds.'

'Perfect Daka. The stump and roots were to remain.' The King further explained.

'I know King Nemfukwe. And bound with iron and bronze bands. Surrounding the base with tender grass.'

'And the meaning Daka?' asked the King.

Daka hesitated. He feared that the dream's meaning would trouble the King. 'I wish the events seen in the dream foreshadow another my Chief, and not you.'

'Fear not. I am a man, a warrior, and a ruler. The ruler of the most potent kingdom on earth!' The King took umbrage but still maintained composure.

Daka swallowed dry and spoke. 'The tree is you my Chief. As you just spoke, you are great and strong. You will be driven from human society, cut down like the Mopane and forced to live among the wild animals that have been dispersed. You will forage for grass. Seven periods of time, the number of large limbs, will pass as you live this way until you realize that someone greater than you exists. The trunk and roots remain. Your kingdom will come back when you learn the lesson of vulnerability. Do the will of Him who rules over all of us, love others more than self, power, and strength. That will ensure that you will always prosper. Stay strong like a mighty Mopane, but humble, loving, and giving. Do not change and you will be cut to a stump, raised, and burned in the eternal fires.'

Students, some of you know the end result of this tale. A year to the day the King walked upon the escarpment. He looked out across his great land. He took pride in the beautiful sites he believed he created and reveled in his Royal

Palace's glory. While praising his achievements, a voice called down to him from the heavens.

'This message is for you. Nemfukwe the Elder, you no longer rule this kingdom. Look one last time. You will be driven from human society. You will live on the veldt with the wild animals and will eat grass like a water buffalo. Seven periods of time will pass while you live this way. Pride, greed, and arrogance have become your curse. You must learn that the most high Chief rules over all of the earth, even over you. He gives to them what He wishes to give. I wish to give you a lesson. Hopefully others will learn from what you have not.'

That same moment, when the voice broke the breezes of the mountains, judgment was fulfilled. Nemfukwe the Elder left, by force of the heavens, human society. He ate the bitter grass, his hair grew long like the wildebeest, his nails clawed like vultures' talons. The Chief's mind demented as he began to rant, rage, and slobber like a rabid jackal. When his time finally elapsed, sanity returned. The Elder fell to his knees praising, honoring, and worshiping the most High One's voice. The King had been restored to the head of his kingdom.

'Professor, professor. That brings us full circle doesn't it? Back to the Elder's grandchildren and the writing on the wall?'

'Yes it does Ms. Precious. The human like finger wrote upon the banquet wall, near Nemfukwe's lampstand. The King saw the hand. He paled with fright. His knees did not hold the terror of his body.'

'What does this mean?' He ordered his wise men to explain.

'Whoever reads the sign will be elevated to purple robes and given royal honor. A gold chain will be your symbol of the third-highest rank within my kingdom.'

Man after man attempted to understand the words. Each failed, causing the King to grow more alarmed, frustrated, and angry.

'Son. Don't be afraid. Long live the King!' spoke the Queen Mother. 'I know of an old man who, during my father's reign, was found to have insight, understanding, and wisdom like the gods. Your grandfather, the Elder, made this now ancient one chief over all the magicians, shamans, enchanters, and fortunetellers. This man, Daka, possesses exceptional abilities, having been imbued with divine knowledge. Call for him. He will comprehend the wall writing.'

'You heard the Queen Mother. Search the land for this old man. Bring him to me, I demand it!'

The King's men found Daka in the lower hills of Kilimanjaro. The ancient one enjoyed communing with his Creator and living close to nature. The forests were his home, the animals his friends, and the heavens his sanctuary.

'I will come,' spoke Daka to the Chief's advisor.

'Are you Daka, one of the exiles brought from Makuni Village by my grandfather, the Elder?'

'I am the one.' Daka spoke with great humility.

'I have heard of your wisdom, insights, and understanding. The spirits of above reside within you, the Queen my mother tells me. My so-called men of knowledge seem to have very little, especially when it comes to my present need.'

The King explained his dilemma and the rewards for a solution.

Daka refused. 'Keep your gifts. I seek no rewards. The one who has gifted me with revelation and insight gave your predecessors glory and honor. They did as they pleased. Their arrogance and pride were met by being dethroned and stripped of all honor and glory. The Elder was banished from society, forced to live like an animal, and made dumb. He learned from whom the true ruling powers come. You knew all this! Yet you follow in the Elder's footsteps. You've defied your Lord.

You have used heavens implements to sip wine and then melted many to create unholy images to idolize and worship. Now you have called down a message from the sky; your face expresses the fear that fills your very soul.'

'Please Daka. Leave me in suspense no longer. I must know the meaning behind those wall words, cried out the Chief whose fear stepped into terror.

'And know you will, all too well! *Mene* – numbered as in the few remaining days of your reign. *Tekel* – weighed since you have not measured up. *Parsin* – divided and given to the Lozi and Puku.'

Immediately Daka was garbed in purple robes and presented with a gold chain, the third highest rank in the land. That same night, Nemfukwe was killed. Students, as you can see, the historical facts ring true, even today. The prophetic dreams have now come again. History repeats itself many times over. How many of us have experienced the supernatural events of the last decade when traveling to Southern Luangwa game reserve. Yes, we are accustomed to the many creatures that roam the savanna. But just as we have familiarity with Luangwa's species, we have now come upon creatures that speak to the supernatural, the unknown, the dark side of existence.

Daka's visions, his dreams, were not for his time but for ours. The mathematicians of Daka's time calculated a date, the twenty-first century, for the events in the wise man's vision to come to fruition. Our math department has done the same number crunching. The twenty-first seems to be the key century for occurrences of the bizarre, unusual, and the most evil to begin.

Just the other evening, I took my family to Chibembe. We walked along the Luangwa River. In the night sky, below the Southern Cross an image of a man appeared. He had been wounded in his wrists and ankles. He held a feeding trough containing an infant. The stars began to run. My grandchildren said they were crying. The moon, at first, illuminated the grey black clouds from behind the billowy puffs. An army of sinister beings appeared above. Eventually that Legion obscured the entire yellow orb. All went black and all fell silent.

The Luangwa ceased to flow. The winds refused to move the smallest jacaranda petal. The animals hid. Daka's four beasts approached us from out of the black night. They, the creatures, challenged the innocence of our young.

'The battle begins today!' They spoke in unison. Their breath reeked of carrion, the human kind.

'We will have no mercy on those who do not follow us. Nemfukwe's golden image did not work to commit all of humanity to honor him. All knees did not bend. That will change today! Kneel and a live – stand and die. Submit and live – rebel and die. Relinquish and have a life – resist and perish. Destruction will arrive like sand through the hourglass, slow and deliberate. Pain will be the avatar that will replace those happy faces. Buried, like a hiker under an ice flow, will you and those who do not genuflect be, forever aware of the ill-gotten reward of choice.'

My family and I looked at each other. We heard of such apparitions but never encountered them in personal conversation. Then, as methodically as the evil transformation took place, this scene at Chibembe went back to its natural state.

Children being children say the darndest things. Speaking of the sinister. 'They're so cute!'

To view the world and those in the world through the eyes of children can be a blessing. Yes, in life there are all sorts of views and interpretations derived from seeing the same earthly forms. That's what makes each person so unique."

Bob realized that he was not in his classroom, the one at the University of Zambia, but on Burk Avenue.

"Bob! Bob! Are you okay?" asked AJ.

"Yes. I'm looking at your clouds and the apparitions in the sky. I believe the time has arrived."

"Dad!" yelled out Elizabeth. "You mean the beasts?"

Bob answered. "Yes. Just like Daka envisioned. Decades after the Elder's dream, Daka had an unusual night vision of his own. He took a stylus in hand and began to inscribe the scenes on clay tablets. The time was just on a night like this. Daka gazed above, like we are doing now. The sky presented dark blood like crimson swirling clouds. The seas raged. Listen!"

The family hushed. The Atlantic could be heard making sounds like the sea had never done before.

"Moans, pain, suffering," noticed Josephine. "I think the ocean is sick," she continued.

Jen added, "The wind gales, worse than four Nor'easters combined. You're right Jojo. Someone or something experiences great distress."

"Yes family. Look!" called out Bob. "The beasts. Daka's beasts! Could it be? Nemfukwe's lion but with eagle wings."

"Bob, I'm afraid," Elizabeth gathered up her children and went to her father.

"Don't worry mom. If he comes near you, I'll open up a can of whoop ass on him."

"AJ, where did you hear that?" chided Gigi.

"Bob and I heard the phrase on wrestling. Steve Austin opens up cans of whoop ass on his opponents, "added AJ.

"Bob. See what you started," Jen had a point. "I thought we were having no more wrestling."

"Sorry Jen girl. Look!" Bob attempted to divert the attention on the can to the trouble in hand.

"A 'lion bird.' The wings are being ripped from the creature. That monstrosity has no hands, only wings. That miscreant is running on its back paws like a human. Its mouth is trying to say something." Elizabeth backed away. Then the thing vanished.

"Did you see mommy?"

"I saw Josephine."

"No. I mean what it said. 'You who have seen will see no more. I'm not sure what that means but that's spooky."

The second beast appeared to the Burk Avenue family. The same as appeared to Daka over 2000 years before.

"A bear," called out Gigi. "It's chewing on three ribs and trying to speak. Listen!"

"I rise up today, after millennia. I've been dormant, now I'm ordered by the dark one to devour the flesh of many people." Then the entity disappeared.

The family stood, transfixed, motionless, with the exception of their eyes resting upon AJ and Josephine. The third creature rose into the heavens from the fog that hung over the back bays. The image appeared to be that of a leopard. Four birdlike wings were attached to its back. The beast also had four heads. The monster possessed great authority and presents. The creature quickly got the attention of our group. The many mouths were gnawing the air as though attempting to ingest any living being that occupied modern-day Earth. The being quickly vanished.

The fourth and final monstrosity, more terrifying, more dreadful, and stronger than the others rose above Nanny's home. That entity began to crush and devour humanity with its huge iron teeth. The bits of mankind that escaped the creature's bite: legs, arms, torsos, heads and so forth were scattered about eventually to be trampled beneath the monster's feet. The beast stood in stark contrast to the first three, having ten horns.

"Look Gigi," shouted Jojo. "A small horn is growing in the front of that thing's head. The hand that wrote on the wall of Nemfukwe's kraal, the one Bob talked about in his book, it's ripping out three horns so that the little guy can fit. The small horn has eyes." Josephine became super animated.

"And a mouth too." yelled out AJ.

A voice invaded the protection that the home at 344 provided. The arrogant little horn atop the beast's head bellowed out its degree.

"I am the final authority. I shall destroy those three that preceded me. Even though the visions say they will live and I will die in the fire that belief will not come to pass." The fourth beast left.

Without hesitation Bob knew what needed to be done. Jen, everyone's Gigi, knew what her husband had in mind. The ever constant battle between evil and good rest always in the hands of the innocent. Only in the unspoiled can a cure-all, an antidote, an elixir foment the forces of good to create the wherewithal to defeat such sinister beings.

Having lifeguard at the beaches for many years, Bob knew the power of sand, wind, sea, surf, sky, and horizon. The family filled up the blue Chevy venture minivan and drove to the beach at Higbee. This shoreline, during Bob's boyhood days, stood in isolation and obscurity to all but the very astute locals of the island. Tourists could not find the secreted entrance, through the woods, that led to the great water's edge where the almighty Atlantic met the vast Delaware Bay.

Mysteries of a spiritual nature loomed throughout the shore's environs. Even now, only a handful of old timers knew the many secrets of Higbee, Diamond, The Point, and Concrete Ship beaches. Tonight would be a lesson well learned by the entire family. In their forty-two years of marriage Jen had heard only a fraction of the lore that her husband experienced at this section of their summer resort.

The couple, totally in love, often visited the beaches. Gigi understood, as a loving wife would, that some things a man and his mistress, in Bob's case the sea, keep confidential until that perfect time for sharing arrives. This was the time and now, Gigi wasn't sure if she wished to know or not.

A word had not been spoken during the twenty minute ride to Higbee. Bob did put in some favorite CDs from Styx, the Doobie Brothers, and ended up with the score from *Phantom of the Opera*. There appeared to be a ritual method to his madness. The night stood inky. Only through years of experience did the van know the turns, landmarks, and limb obscured paths to a parking area above the great beach.

Bob unlocked the van doors. He opened each one in a systematic order.

"I can hear the…" Jojo had been immediately cut off by cries, shrill cries from out of the dark.

The wails could've been a cat in the night or an infant's panic. No matter the case, the cacophony did its job. All fell silent again. Then, as if by hypnosis, Bob began to quickly and nimbly traverse the thickets with the family attempting to keep pace. Something or someone drew him through the sand paths like a guide tracking big-game in Luangwa.

The mighty sea and the bay could be discerned from a distance away: sound, smell, and taste lured the group to the banquet of emotional ups and downs. The roar of the crashing surf increased as the family approached the final dune. Bob reached the precipice, first reaching out a hand to Elizabeth. She had also been here many times before and knew that the steep incline to the water's edge, from the top of the dune, stood two stories below from where they stood.

"Bob's on a mission," whispered Gigi not wishing to disturb the night.

The elder husband picked up his gait, ran down the dune, passed the sandy shore, and began to climb the rock pile which jutted out deep into the sea. He and the family gazed out upon the great expanse of water. The clouds lowered, almost smothering. The sea churned, wanting to sate itself with humans.

"He's transfixed," Elizabeth told her mom.

Without warning, and with Bob only expecting, a strange scaly creature rose up out of the surf. A sea serpent of astronomical proportions showed itself. The long-necked, opalescent-colored, red forked-tongued, bright scarlet rooster-combed, blue-eyed Dragon breathed Puccini-like musical notes from its crocodile-like snout.

"Bob! Hello! Seems like the time has come."

Bob nodded an affirmative while Jojo asked AJ, "Grand Pop knows him?"

The sea dragon looked to the family and then to the sky. An aberration appeared, the Southern Cross in the northern sky. Pinned to the structure, the man child, but this time badly wounded. The figure looked basically as it did in Chibembe, still carrying the trough in one hand and the sword of judgment in the other. This time though, the feeding tub stood empty.

"I see Bob, you brought the family as I instructed you to do many many years ago. I told you that grandchildren would come."

"Yes. I've had to live with that all this time. I can't. I won't allow it." Bob teared.

"You believed. That's good. They came to your daughter," said the serpent.

"And that's where they shall stay. She believed too and so did her mother, my wife. We will not allow this," Bob explained most forcefully.

"But in life, everything has a price," the dragon spoke calmly.

"That price is too high. Take me. The price is too high!" Bob began to sob.

"Now the time has come to collect and to pay Bob." The leviathan raised its oversized side fins splashing and soaking both Bob and his family. They had no idea of the price that one pays for dreams fulfilled, horizons gained, and wishes granted. Prayers are always answered but many times not in the way the kneeling one asks or hopes.

In the midst of the discussion thunderous claps of lightning raced across the ebon sky. The flashes could be seen on the faces of those who stood by the water's edge. Then the earth began to tremble.

"Nice effect. Don't you think Bob?" spoke the creature.

'You always had a flair for the dramatic," answered Bob.

"Yells bells, vectors sectors, telepathy shellepethy, laser mazer, vision collision, translate eradicate the evil that confronts the world. Have some fun answer the pun. The presents will not only solidify the past but our future as well. Kids! Kids! Over here!"

Josephine and AJ walked upon the rock jetty toward Bob.

"Hey, I have a couple of riddles for you to solve. The fate of our entire planet depends, and I don't mean adult diapers, I mean really depends on your answers. The power that you will receive to defeat the beasts will come with correct responses. And you do not have to form them into a question. Ready?" spoke the dragon.

The two children looked to Bob in confusion. He smiled. They had confidence in that loving response.

"Ready confetti," both AJ and Jojo answered.

"How did you know my name?"

AJ jumped on that. "You look Italian, you're a rainbow of color, and you throw a lot of sh..."

"Don't say it AJ!" interrupted Bob.

"Sorry Bob. Confetti – your ideas can be thrown around to bring joy to all. How's that for throwing the bull, Confetti!?"

"Very good children. That was the first riddle or test. My name. Not the dung thingy. Remember, if you fail one, you fail all. That means no more you, or they, anymore. See? That's how the game goes. Now for the next pun. With the economy down, what did the garbage collector say about his business?"

"Oh silly Confetti. That's too easy – it's picking up!"

"Jojo, you are not only very cute but very smart. I hear you don't like subtraction."

"Who told you that!"

"Bob did," answered Confetti.

"You are causing trouble Mister Dragon," shouted Bob to his friend. "I said Jojo prefers addition. She changes the signs to 'plus' because Jojo is a positive thinker."

"My bad. I didn't mean to cause a large numerical problem in your family. I won't multiply the issues with more talk that will lead to a division among you. In this area, within the perimeter of the bay, I'm known for my acute slant on math. I present an angle that no one has considered."

"Mister Confetti. You're going off on a tangent and speaking in circles. The volume in your voice can wake the dead," reminded Bob.

"Sorry family. A good percentage of what I say can be had at a fraction of one's mental attention. But if you insist, I'll do a total 180°

turnabout and never eat pie again, even though my favorite is 22/7ths." Confetti didn't wish to cease with his mathematical humor. He understood that if it weren't for laughter all would be crying endlessly.

"Confetti! Joseph!" yelled out Jen. "I can't take any more of this Three Stooges-like inane banter about math. Please. Did the children pass or not? And can we go home?"

Confetti turned to Gigi. "Miss Jen. You're in quite a snit. A few more quips and the test will be concluded. Children. What did the Doctor do when the ailing actor overacted?"

"Ugh!" sighed Jen.

Dragon cut off Gigi. "Who wants to answer this one? Okay. Jojo?"

"Cured the ham!"

"Are you satisfied Mister Confetti?" asked Elizabeth. "Can my children now do what needs to be done, so the doing can be over and done with soon?"

Confetti knew the angst that the family experienced. That gave him reason for the silly antics to continue a tad more. Therefore Confetti attempted light humor to alleviate some of the fear and trepidation, of the possibility of losing the young ones to the beasts that could haunt the adults over the course of the trial.

"Those kiddies are too smart. I won't ask them about the thousand dollar store's first day being a grand success or the winning tennis doubles partners who wore the same outfits being game, set, and match! Or that lefty joined the school newspaper because he was 'write' minded. Hey, some in rapid fire. What happened when both employees wanted the last cup of coffee?"

AJ answered quickly. "A fight brewed."

"What the bride did at the makeup table." Confetti thought he had them.

"She blushed," shouted out Josephine.

"What's another name for a lullaby?"

Both children answered, "Rock music."

"When the acupuncture worked, the patient said it was?" Confetti felt that this was a tough one. "Think Josephine. Take your time. I gave you a hard one."

"A jab well done, duh," Jojo smiled.

Josephine's answer caused the serpent to roll over and over, in the water, from laughter. Bob plopped to a sitting position, wiping the tears from his laughing face.

"Oh brother," was all that Elizabeth could say.

But the trick that Confetti had planned worked. Everyone was at ease while the transformation of the two children took place. The powers were implanted by the figure on the Southern Cross. Jojo and AJ were prepared to do battle. Evil against good would be the order of the day.

The two were given the wherewithal to compete against the beasts. The price was great. But the final power gifted to the brother and sister, by the entity attached to the Southern Cross atrophied at exponential speed. In the meantime the four beasts in Daka's dream filled the sky. The fourth monstrosity, the one with the many horns, began to attack the stars that had come out, upon the children's transformation.

The main horn, the one that just recently erupted upon the head of the hideous creature butted everything in its way. The stars shattered, sending spear-like projectiles to earth. The lances of light pierced wildlife on both land and sea. The carnage began in earnest with the beast being the aggressor and early victor. No one could stand against the beast nor help the victims.

Bob, on seeing the inception of nightmares coming to fruition, yelled to his family.

"Shelter yourselves. I have the children!"

Two special beams directed by the beast and iridescent purple, traveled toward the two young recruits. Bob gathered his grandchildren in his arms. His back caught both blasts. AJ and Josephine felt the sudden pain by the expression on their grandfather's face.

"Run children. You'll be safe upon the dune. Run!" Bob shushed the two from the rock pile and turned to the beast. "You did not succeed. Our two live to fight another day. They shall overcome what you have in store for the world."

His last words ended as a lava flow of blood emanated from his mouth. Bob fell dead upon the jetty. He lay, face down, in a pool of crimson vomit. Another light spear, hitting Jen on the thigh, stopped her from running to her husband, along with the grabbing hands of her grandchildren which also dragged their mother toward safety. Elizabeth had also been wounded on the left shoulder as well.

"Mommy. The dunes."

"Gigi, listen to Bob."

"He knows what's best."

The phrases came rapid fire, like the rays that prevented mother and daughter from getting to father and husband. Bob's advice proved correct. Once upon the precipice, the attack could not penetrate the surroundings. From atop the enormous barrier of sand, the family look toward the rocks. Bob's body, in that red puddle, displayed his back wounds oozing the same deep crimson liquid in which he lay. The adults still attempted to move toward him but the shower of lightning spears were too great.

"No! He's in a better place," spoke Jojo.

"We must listen to him. Stay here. We're safe," advised the now, man of the house.

The children knew what the adults failed to realize.

'The dune has life mommy, "spoke AJ. And life it did have. For the giant mound began to shift and undulate beneath the family's feet.

"All is fine. Stay!" ordered the sandy shore. "You may feel more comfortable holding on to a scrub pine. No need to, just for peace of mind. You humans are an interesting lot you are."

The huge dune uplifted itself, like us well in the ocean, rolling toward the home on Burk Avenue with the family "surfing" the sand wave. Every space that the silica mass occupied became free from the beastly attack. A protective invisible shield hovered above.

"Don't cry Gigi. He's fine! Josephine hugged her grandmother hard around the waist.

"Things always look tragic during the storm. Life is a casting off. Bob may look dead, may be dead, is dead. But he's fine! Like this baby mountain said, 'trust.'" AJ spoke some words of wisdom and then added, "Mommy, you always told us that love is the best medicine. If you really believe those words, then our grandfather is cured. He has no pain, no suffering, no hurt. He's at peace."

Jen and Elizabeth's puzzlement over the children's calm, quelled the adults tears.

Elizabeth asked, "What's happened to you two?"

"Nothing mom," answered Jojo. "I can see pictures in my head that show me everything will all be fine in the end. Maybe not how we wish and hope something to end but the One's end. Wait. Your shoulder. Blood." Jojo reached to her mother and before her tiny little fingers could touch Elizabeth's Philadelphia Eagles sweatshirt the wound ceased to seep, began to close, and healed immediately. The fleece still remained holed and stained at the entry spot of the light spear. Elizabeth looked to her young one not being able to figure out what had just happened.

"Gigi, your leg." One glance from AJ put Jen's thigh back to the way it was, pre-lightning spear.

"Could you..." AJ answered before his grandmother could finish.

Then he continued to speak. "We can do that stuff we just did. We can't make the dead come back. Dead is dead. I'm not sure what we can or can't do. I hear a voice in my heart telling me all kinds of things. It's like one of my remote control cars. I am the cream-colored Mustang. Somebody is working the buttons and levers."

"Me too mom. What AJ just said. That's me too. And the voices are saying we need to get ready to play. Play against those sky people, the bad ones. Whoever wins, wins forever."

The family quickly arrived back to Burk Avenue. The sky, ominous and dank set the stage for the final conflagration. The day of doom had arrived. The fall season at the seashore transforms from a Mardi Gras atmosphere to a cemetery-like setting. Nature reclaims itself after being used, abused, and tossed away.

On this particular September day, nature became captured by the promise of Nemfukwe's wall and Daka's dreams. The earth trembled from the evil that the beasts disseminated.

'Hey! Hungry?" asked Nanny as the family walked through the doorway. The old battleship gray painted wooden framed screen door slammed behind AJ.

"Where's Bob?"

The lack of a response and the tears from the adults told Nanny Gert what she already knew. Like the strong patriarch she proved to be, the clan leader went to them and sat each one at the kitchen table. After preparing tea and Dakota wax cookies she sat down to hear the entire story.

Then the ninety-six year old woman spoke. "We came here in 1912. Ours was the only house on this side of Burk. Suddenly, the urbanites discovered the beauty and solace of the island. After the depression, prosperity and greed became the American Dream. Now we reap, in 2013, over 100 years after our arrival here, the results of such behavior. Jen, your leg! Elizabeth, your shoulder! Let me look at them."

"We're fine."

"No you're not." Gert looked.

"You are."

"That's part of the story Nanny," Jen began to tell her grandmother how the healings happened.

"Just like I've studied." Nanny was a student of the chosen words. "I see that the times have arrived."

Suddenly, and without warning the skies exploded, "Pooo! Kaboom!"

Running out the back door, the family looked to the sounds. The winged lion, Eagle-like, bear, bird flying leopard, and multi-headed horned serpent had taken possession of the first and second strata of the heavens. Angel like beings, flying fish of all species, and birds of every genus attempted to defend mankind. The evil entities came out of the West, causing a land so swiftly that they were difficult to discern.

The horned slug headed toward the gaggle of Angels which stood upon a series of clouds. The hideous one rushed the winged spirits in a hate-filled rage. The delicate creatures charged the multi-headed beast, disengaging a number of its horns. They grew back larger, more ferocious, and much deadlier than the ones that had been pulled out of its heads. The heinous one countered with a flowing series of toxic expectorant which temporarily sedated the slight ones.

Knocking them off the clouds, the heads began to mangle each falling Angel. Blood, viscera, and entrails rained down to earth, peppering those who watched. No one could rescue the cloud protectors from the power of the fourth beast. The more it ate of its carrion, the more it grew in strength and ferocity. Each horn lost, grew back four more. The other beasts gained courage from the fourth.

They began to attack all the defenders of the innocent. The beasts laid down the gauntlet, challenging the commander of the highest realm.

"We shall sacrifice your entire forces, your so-called Omni One. Your temple shall and will be totally destroyed. Our mark will be indelibly branded upon each of your innocent ones. They will know to whom they belong. Evil will rule the entire universe."

With those promises, the Legion of the filth, foul, festered, flagitious phantasm dictated to the One, "truth was overthrown!" The beasts began to succeed in everything they did.

"Listen Gigi. I hear talking." stated AJ.

"Over there," Jen pointed to a spot in Ottens Harbor where two prophet- like looking men, in robes, stood. They walked upon the murky green water.

"How long will these events of Daka's vision last?" one of the prophets asked.

The other turned to the sailing ship that approached and she questioned, "How long will the rebellion insist on sacrifice?"

The male figure asked another question. "How long will the Temple of One remain under siege and heaven's Army be trampled?"

The sailing ship came close to the walking upon water figures. Lashed to the mizzen, the figure that had once been attached to the Southern Cross, answered.

"2300 nights, then all will be made right."

The battle, as they spoke, continued overhead. The family did not realize that throughout the planet war occupied every space in every sector of the sky. Fear, terror, hate, and evil took hold of all that ever touched good. The worldly began to win with man, woman, and child being branded into the Army of the beasts. Family fought and slaughtered family. Friend betrayed friend. Greed, avarice, and covetousness became life's avatar. Then, the figure upon this sailing ship called "Endeavor," attempted to speak.

The voice bellowed out, "I've sent Daka to tell you the meaning of what you witness."

The old Fulani prophet, visionary, and warrior from centuries past appeared from the marshy reeds of the back bay.

"It's him." spoke Aunt Ida who had been on the Dell working on another anthropological thesis to be presented at the United Nations. "Daka has come back from the place in which he rested. The words come now."

"Sons of man," Daka pointed, from the distance, toward Jojo and AJ. "You two." They looked toward the figure. "Understand this. The things which you see now do not bode well for our planet. My times have come and gone. I rest, like grandfather rests. We have made our life's statements. Only time will, as you two know, make life better. Do not look to the past, that action can mire you in darkness. Glance, yes! But do not stare. The quick look ensures never forgetting but guarantees nothing about repeating the ills of lost generations. You two know why you have been summoned. The visions you see relate to the time of the end!"

Nanny Gert, the keeper of the family Word, knew end times. She fainted. Daka came to her as she lay with her face upon the ground. He raised her with a touch and brought Gert to her feet.

"I've come to reaffirm what the old woman and two young ones know about the coming events that will lead up to the time of wrath. What you see pertains to one end but the inception of something unfamiliar and new. The beasts require no explanation. You know who and what they are, for they all live within. Those who come behind their evil force are not strangers to your intellect. They've come to divide and conquer as the old adage suggests. They speak to only the first segment of adversarial attacks.

When their evil transgressions upon earth reach their height, a more ferocious and sinister one will rise up against innocence. She will become strong, but not by her own power alone. The woman will cause a shocking amount of destruction. Those who live to see the actions will look with mouths agape, hearts palpitating, and throats as dry as the Sahara. Leaders will be destroyed. The righteous will be devastated. This female will be a master of deception. The more chaos, suffering, and pain the woman distributes the more arrogant and vile she will become. Without warning the masses shall be destroyed if they refuse to bow down. Look over there." Daka pointed to the figure who stood upon the vessel anchored in Ottens Harbor.

"This she devil will have the audacity to even confront Him. Why? Because **SHE FEEDS OFF THE GREED OF HUMANITY.** No human power will be able to stop her. The days, 2300, ring true. The time for the prophecy to reach fulfillment rests upon that number. When has the calendar count begun? The answer to that question will answer many others."

With those final words Daka walked backward, disappearing into the tall marsh grass. The adults of the family took heed of his words. They spoke nothing, having faith and trust in the young. All that month and the next, the battles continued. Humanity rebelled, many individuals broke promises, and society disobeyed the commands.

The woman grew in strength because of the corruption of mankind. Iniquity and trespasses were the archetypes that the masses lived by and reacted to while AJ and Jojo gathered forces. Almost to the human, each refused to listen to the prophet's voice. They did not cover their shameful faces as each person attempted to make covert deals with both evil and good. They wished to "hedge their bets" so they played both sides. But they failed to realize, that even alone, two people are always watching.

Many admitted to transgression but still had the audacity to face the One, believing that He or She, if you wish to be idiotically politically correct, could be deceived. The beasts enjoyed watching the show. They used the time-tested excuse, "but everyone else is doing it!" Then the fourth beast appeared, above where Daka walked from the reeds.

"We do wrong and wallow in the iniquity. We will forever rebel against Him." The sinister one pointed toward the figure upon the deck of "Endeavor." "We, and I speak for self-centered, selfish, egotistical man, scorn all of your commands and regulations. We will not listen! We refuse to listen! Shame does not affect us, nor does guilt... Who dares interrupt me!" shouted the demon.

From all corners of the world voices of suffering, pain, and anguish could be heard.

"The Word has been kept. Woe is us." The Earth's humanity began to cry out for relief. Time had expired, no more sand remained in the hourglass.

" Every curse against us, written in the Law of Rennis has come true. Have mercy upon us, oh Great One. Our truth fell short."

The pleas for compassion and forgiveness landed on deaf ears. The disaster that had been prepared centuries earlier had begun.

"We did not obey. Please give us another chance. Rescue your people." Deaf ears once again met the entreats of the people. "We implore you. Here your servants. Listen, we beg you."

AJ and Josephine looked at each other. They knew that the challenge ahead of them stood monumental. Then, the figure upon the sail ship spoke, confirming what Confetti had endowed to the two young ones.

"I'm here to give you understanding and insight. You are the precious ones to whom the power has been bestowed. Listen carefully to learn the meanings of all you need to know. You two have been imbued with the strength and ability to end the rebellion, to put a finale to treason, to confirm righteousness upon those who will join you in the battle.

All this vile materialism will be replaced with strong defenses, even in the most perilous of times. Floods, wars, misery will be commonplace to purge the evil times of the malignant stench of most of humanity. But beware, the one who comes in sheep's clothing, she will perform heinous and horrendous deeds. The defiler will pour out putrefied palaver, pandemic pestilence, pusillanimous patricide, and purulent puissance. There will never be such disaster as that which comes.

You two children have been given insight and understanding. The moment you began to give of yourself to others, you became precious to them. I will leave you to protect that which I leave behind. You and only you can accomplish the change which I bestow and desire. The end looms near, misery I decree to that end. Now look upon this vision," demanded the figure.

"Mom, see at the bottom of the bay. Sunset Lake has never looked so beautiful," commented Josephine.

"A man under the water. His robe is cinched with a belt of gold." AJ described the scene, for the adults did not see the vision but knew something transpired by the "green out" around the lake. A deep verdure tinted the sky, the landscape, and the water.

"Family," continued AJ, "his body looks like a ruby glowing in an amber fire. His eyes are two torches sitting upon a face of perfect peace. Look! Look! His limbs shine like polished bronze. His voice commands."

Everyone, from the figure's first words flowing from the water's bed, had been knocked to the ground. His words made the earth tremble. A hand reached out of the bay riffling the surface. The fingers touched each of the young ones, lifting the two children up, onto their feet.

"You are most precious to me. Listen carefully to what I have to say. Stand and be strong."

"AJ, I'm afraid."

"Me too sis. But we can't let them know." AJ referred to his family, wishing to spare them undue worry.

"Do not fear! From the first day, you have done what all should have been doing. You humbled yourself. Your requests were not for you but to help others. They have been heard.

You're only children. Those who received should have known better. They have lived many years but were blind where you, eyes of such a short view, could see. We have been blocked in coming to you sooner by their greed. But we are now here. The Southern Cross, Confetti, and now the One from beneath the sea who speaks to you have arrived. I now say these things about your people and a time yet to come."

"Hey Mister, stop being so spooky," spoke Jojo. "You knocked us down with that voice of yours, now you pretend to be so serious. What's up with you? Stop scaring us."

The figure reached out again, from the surface of the brackish water. He touched the children upon their foreheads.

"Don't be afraid. There! You feel fine now, right?"

The two nodded in the affirmative.

"Be strong. Be brave. Be encouraged. You are the precious ones."

"Then speak, but not in riddles. We are still kids you know. And yes, we do feel strong and fearless." AJ stood determined.

"You know why your?" spoke the figure.

"If we did, we wouldn't have to have this conversation," offered Josephine.

"I came to prepare for the total cataclysm. Things have gotten so out of hand with these people. Look at the ads on radio, TV, and in the print media. Look at the suicide rate, deaths of the unborn, the increase in therapy sessions and psychiatric drug use, juvenile violence, greed, lust, avarice, and such. Everyone wishes to be Boss Bigshot and super famous and significant. They vie to be richer than Trump and garner more power. Enough has now not become enough. Enjoy the dream not the reality, lives in the hearts of mankind. Miss the now moments for the 'I can't wait to have's.'

They can't get no satisfaction. The lost generation at least knew that they were lost. Not only is the present lost, they don't even realize that they are absent. Nobody knows that they can't be found, that they are nothings, that they are totally insignificant in this industrialized world. Facebook has really shown how low humanity has sunken and what low self-esteem society has. If you don't understand, shame on you; I have no pity for you. The world is in a real big mesh."

"You mean mess, don't you," corrected AJ.

"Yes. When you were a tiny one you said 'mesh' for mess. That was cute, real, and natural. Not like the frauds, phonies, and fakes like we have today."

"You can say that again," spoke Jojo.

So he did. "The world is in a real big mesh…"

"That was a figure of speech sir. I really didn't mean that you needed to say that again. I was supporting, in a roundabout way, what you said."

"I know. I wanted to be funny, break the tension of conflict and doom."

"Ugh!" sighed Josephine.

"The only solution I can see is to have the world erupting chaos, to be broken apart in all bits and pieces. I need to sap the authority, the arrogance, the attitude from them." The figure had planned this long before any inhabitants took over the planet.

"And we do want?" asked AJ.

The gold cinched robe wearer spoke. "What you need to do."

The answer caught Jojo's attention. "That's not a good answer Mister!"

"We need to play, run, and have kid fun. Not save the civilized world," added AJ.

"Nobody promised you that life would be one big gig," explained bay man.

"Mankind messed that up. Perfect man, perfect in every way. What's the matter with kids today?"

"What do you mean by that?" AJ placed his hands on his hips waiting for an answer.

"Sorry. I was recalling *Bye-Bye Birdie* and got carried away. Let me get back to the point. Man is perfect; doing only what man can do. He's totally perfectly self-absorbed. He has made profit his/her God. Pleasure has become her/his life blood. And power he/she wants as his/her sustenance. Humanity has abandoned that moniker 'human,' no more does being humane or having human concerns live in the hearts of our earthly race. Gold and silver, if I may speak metaphorically, have transplanted their souls."

Other publications by Josephine Publishing Press: (charpubpress@aol.com)

THE NURSING HOME: a short play by joey donato ph.d.

AFRICAN FOLK TALES from Matero... by Dr.jol

2012 SAVING THE SPIRIT by Dr. jol

CASTLES OF ROSEMONT by joey donato ph.d.

CARMELLA'S TWINS by joey donato ph.d.

LOVE the problems and the F'n solutions by Dr. Jol

SUBURBAN BRAND by Dr. Jol

SHORT SHORTS by Dr. Jol Ph. D.

VICTORIA a pirate romance by Dr. J D Philip

WORLD WITHOUT END by J D Philip Ph. D. eBook only

HOLY MATRIMONY and LET'S MAKE A MOVE TWO PLAYS by j d Philip ph.d.

THREE NOVELLAS etc. by jol ph.d.

CHRIST'S WOMEN the seven Marys by joey donato ph.d.

GOD MADE "F'n" EASY by dr. jol Ph.D.

UNDER THE SUN by joey donato ph.d.

REIDUNN-VIKING GODDESS by joey donato ph.d.

EL GATO NEGRO- escaping 13 deaths by Marcello Mendoza and Joey Donato

ABSOLVO TE the forgiving and the F ' n forgetting by jol ph.d.

THUNDER SIX from grunt to pilot Viet Nam to Desert Storm by Richard Kessler and J. Liberkowski ph.d.

A GUIDE TO AUTHENTICATING U S PRESIDENTIAL AUTOGRAPHS by Dr. jol

BECKY-from slave to bride by dr.jol

2045-the eternal curse- battling the Legion by dr. jol

These can be purchased from Lulu.com

We also suggest that you please look at the following. If you have enjoyed our authors you'll appreciate their art; www.refindfurnishings.com art by Jol. Be sure to click on the site links. Also, http://mocapa1950.wix.com/refindfurnishings. Thank you from Josephine Publishing Press!

Recommendations, comments, suggestions:
charpubpress@aol.com